Clarence is Flying

Written by Michèle Dufresne
Illustrated by Max Stasiuk

PIONEER VALLEY EDUCATIONAL PRESS, INC.

I am flying
over the house.

2

3

I am flying over the field.

5

I am flying
over the unicorn.

I am flying
over the river.

8

I am flying
over the troll.

I am flying over the mermaid.

I am flying
over the volcano.

I am flying
up, up, up!